To My Wife Miska

a Hungarian folktale
retold & illustrated
by COLOS

the student who became king in spite of himself.

HOLT, RINEHART AND WINSTON
New York   Chicago   San Francisco

Once upon a time, beyond the Glass Mountain, there was a great sea. In this great sea lived a little fish.

On the biggest tooth of this little fish was written this story:

One day a student left home in order to see the world. As he walked along he came upon a field where he found some tiny green balls.

"These can help me some day," thought the student, for he was poor and remembered that his father had often advised him to pick up anything he could that was worth more than a flea. So he picked up the little peas and stuffed them into his pocket.

At nightfall he arrived at the city of the King. Without hesitating, he had himself announced at the palace and asked for some sausages for his evening meal and shelter for the night.

The student was very handsome, had beautiful manners, and spoke very agreeably. The Queen noticed all this and because she had an extremely beautiful daughter of marriageable age, she imagined that perhaps the young man was a prince disguised as a student. She told the King what she was thinking and he agreed with her, so they decided to put the boy to a test in order to find out if he were really the son of a king.

They invited him to stay two days longer at the palace. A very ordinary bed was prepared for him for the night: if he slept well, he was only a student; if not, he was the son of a king.

His room
was in a distant wing
of the palace;
the King posted
a trustworthy man
at the student's window
to report to him on the
young man's conduct.
The student was very tired
and, while undressing,
he clumsily spilled
all of the peas
from his pocket
onto the bed. He began
gathering them up
one by one,
and this occupied him
until daylight.

The King's man was not able to see what kept the student so busy or why he could go to sleep only at daybreak.

Therefore he reported to the King that the guest had hardly slept at all and was very disturbed by his bed. It would seem, then, that he was not used to this kind of bed!

The young man rose and had breakfast. The King asked him if he had had a good night.

"It was rather bad," he answered, "but it's my own fault." From this the King deduced that the young man was sorry he had not admitted he was a prince, and had not been given a bed suitable to his rank.

The next night, they prepared a royal bed for him. The young man, who, the night before, had hardly closed his eyes, fell sound asleep as soon as his head touched the pillow. He budged not an inch until morning. Of course, he had no problem at all with the peas, which, the night before, he had been careful to tie up in his handkerchief.

The next morning, the King's man reported that the guest had spent a very good night. The King and the Queen were now certain that the young man was a prince disguised as a student. Therefore, they began to call him "Your Highness," despite his objections. The Princess, who had never seen so handsome a prince, fell madly in love with him and their marriage was celebrated with great splendor.

They had been married for a year when the old King, putting them both in a carriage, declared that the Prince should take his wife to see his *own* kingdom.

The young man became terribly frightened. What could he do? He fell into a gloomy state and decided that at the first chance he would run away and go back to school.

A few days later, after crossing mountains and plains, the Prince and his Princess arrived at a huge forest. There the young man made his way through the thick trees into a deep ravine. But at the very moment he was about to get rid of his princely clothes and run away, he came face to face with a dragon that had seven heads!

"Who are you? What do you want? What are you doing here?" asked the dragon. The young man told him the whole story and explained that sooner or later he would have to get away.

"Don't run off," said the dragon. "That would be a shame! Go on, and as soon as you leave the forest you will see a large castle on a duck's foot. Enter, settle yourself in with your wife, your dogs, your cats, and your red fish, and live there in peace. But, I warn you, when you feel the castle beginning to turn around, run away quickly; this will mean that I am planning to enter. And if I find you there, it will be the end of you."

The young man then returned to his wife and servants and they went on. As they left the forest, they caught sight of the castle. They went in, settled down, and were wonderfully at home there. They lived in the castle for seven happy years—years so happy that finally the student himself believed he was a king.

On a beautiful fall day near the end of the seventh year, the castle suddenly began to tremble and shake, and then to turn faster and faster. The young man was very sad, and, overwhelmed, he left the place. He wandered about for a long time, until he met an old witch, who said to him,

"What is troubling you, oh King?"

"My trouble," he replied, "is that I am not a king at all, but I have to act like one." And he explained his whole story from the beginning.

"You can be glad you told me everything," the witch said. "I am Batu, Queen of the Tartars, the fiercest enemy of that seven-headed dragon. Do as I say. Have a loaf of bread baked seven times over, and then put it in front of the castle door. This loaf of bread will speak so well to the dragon that he will never disturb you again and the castle will be all yours."

The young man did not have to hear this advice again. He had the loaf of bread baked seven times, and at midnight he had it put at the castle doorstep.

At dawn, with the sun rising in the sky, the dragon appeared. He wanted to go into the castle, but the loaf of bread stopped him.

"Halt! I am the sentinel! You shall not enter without my permission! First you must go through what I have gone through."

"I must get in," said the dragon. "Tell me what I have to do."

The loaf of bread then explained that when she was a seed she had been covered with dirt, had crumbled into dust, started life again, had grown and suffered through the cold, the snow, and the rain — and then, finally, had blossomed.

"Then," she went on, "they harvested me, crushed me, milled me, kneaded me, and finally tossed me into an oven seven times. When you have gone through all that, then and only then can you enter this castle."

The dragon knew that he would never be able to bear so much, and he became so angry that he choked with rage and died on the spot.

From that day on, the young man was Lord of the castle and of all the countryside. After the old King died, he ruled two countries. And if he hasn't himself died yet, he still does.

If I could know before it happened that I could have such good luck I would become a student at once.

COLOS was born in Budapest, Hungary, where he lived until 1956 when he moved to Paris. He remained there until coming to the United States in 1969. His reputation as a uniquely talented graphic artist had already reached this country and his work soon began to appear in American publications such as *The New York Times, Life, Harper's* and *Time*. He is also a photographer and filmmaker.

Colos is an avid collector of postage and legal stamps, old engravings, decals, stickers, drawings and prints, which he incorporates with his own drawings into his collages. *The Student Who Became King in Spite of Himself* is the artist's first book for children. He now makes his home in New York City with his wife, Michèle.